The FARMYARD CAT

Christine Anello
illustrated by Sharon Thompson

Ashton Scholastic

Sydney   Auckland   New York   Toronto   London

For Frank and Joseph Errol

Anello, Christine.
    The farmyard cat.

    ISBN 0 86896 380 1.
    ISBN 0 86896 392 5 (pbk.).
    ISBN 0 86896 393 3 (large ed.).

    1. Cats — Juvenile fiction. I. Thompson, Sharon. II.
    Title.

A823'.3

First published in 1987 by Ashton Scholastic Pty Limited (Inc. in NSW), PO Box 579,
Gosford 2250. Also in Brisbane, Melbourne, Adelaide, Perth and Auckland, NZ.

Typeset by Dovatype, Collingwood.
Printed in Hong Kong
12 11 10 9 8 7 6 5 4 3 2 1   789/80/9

The farmyard cat was out walking. She was very, very, hungry.

She spied the big fat chickens
in the farmyard hen-house.

'I'll get you, chickens!'
hissed the cat.
'I'll get you!'
She sprang high
and clung on to
the hen-house wire.

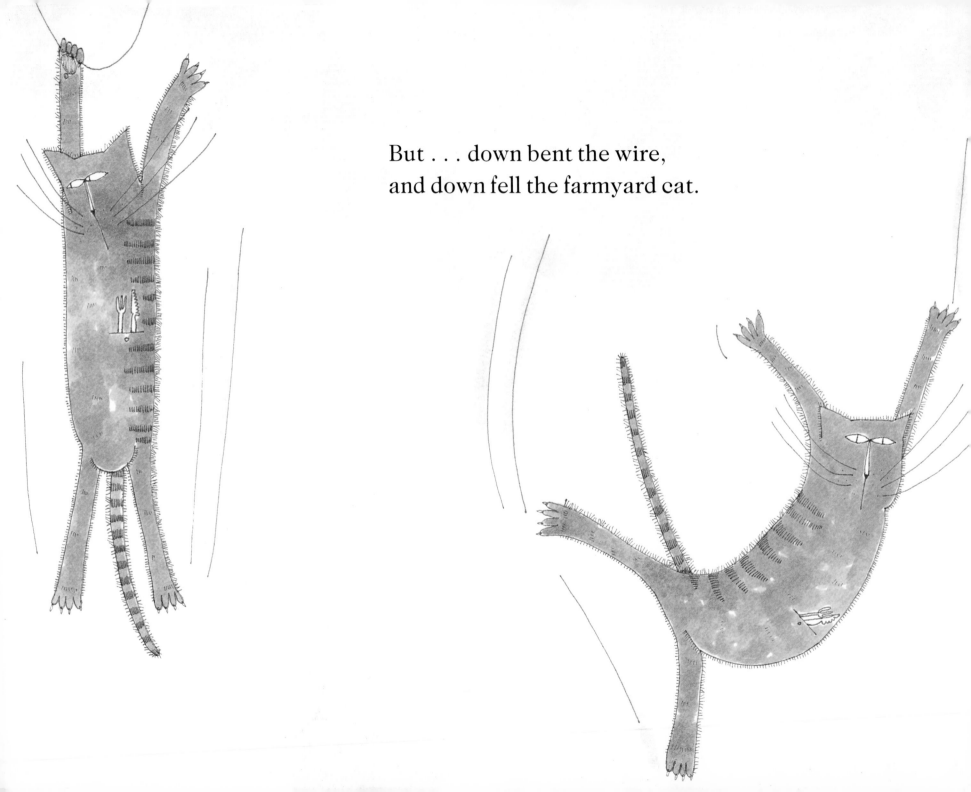

But . . . down bent the wire,
and down fell the farmyard cat.

With claws stretched w-i-d-e,
she landed . . .

. . . on top of the farmyard dog.

The farmyard dog was very angry.
He began to chase the farmyard cat.

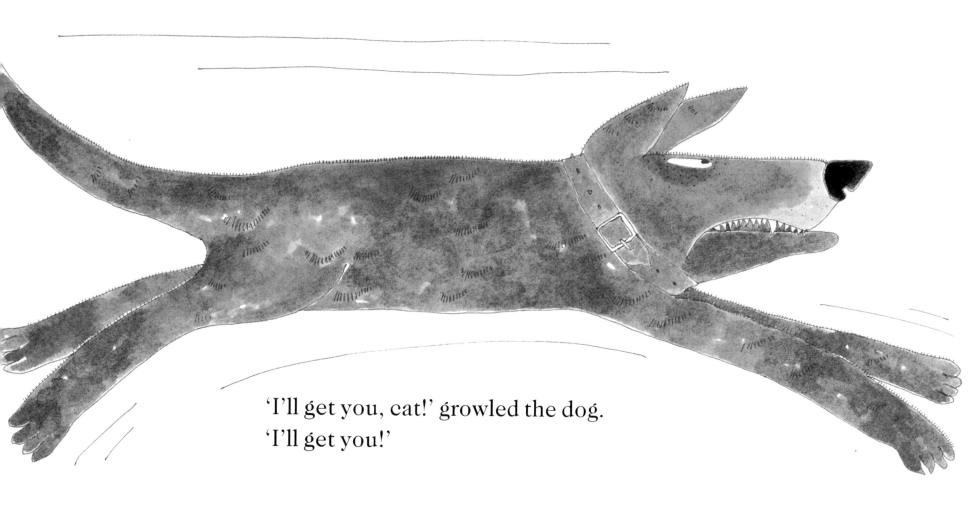

'I'll get you, cat!' growled the dog.
'I'll get you!'

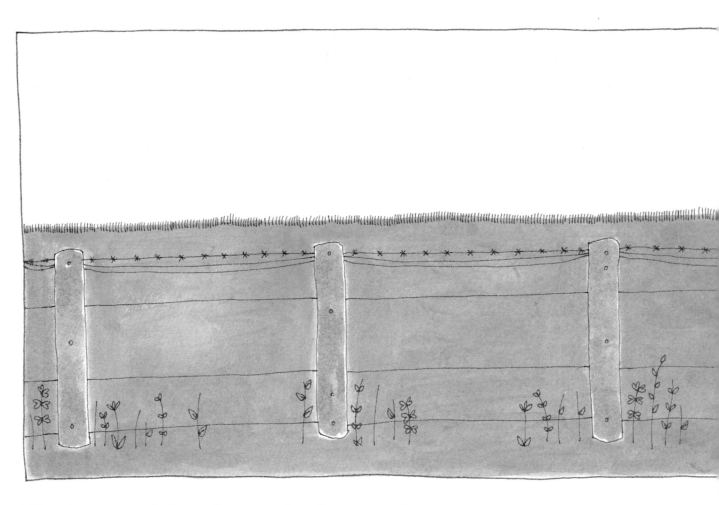

The farmyard dog chased the farmyard cat
under the paddock fence.

They woke . . .

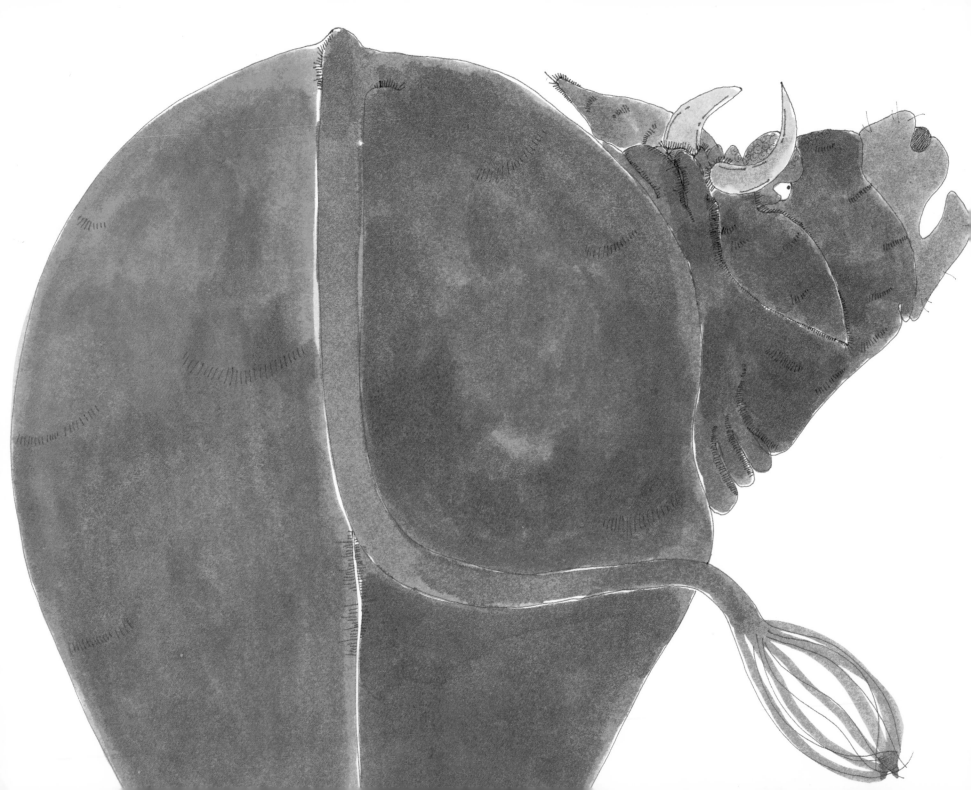

. . . the farmyard bull.

The farmyard bull was very angry.
He began to chase the farmyard cat.

'I'll get you, cat!' bellowed the bull.
'I'll get you!'

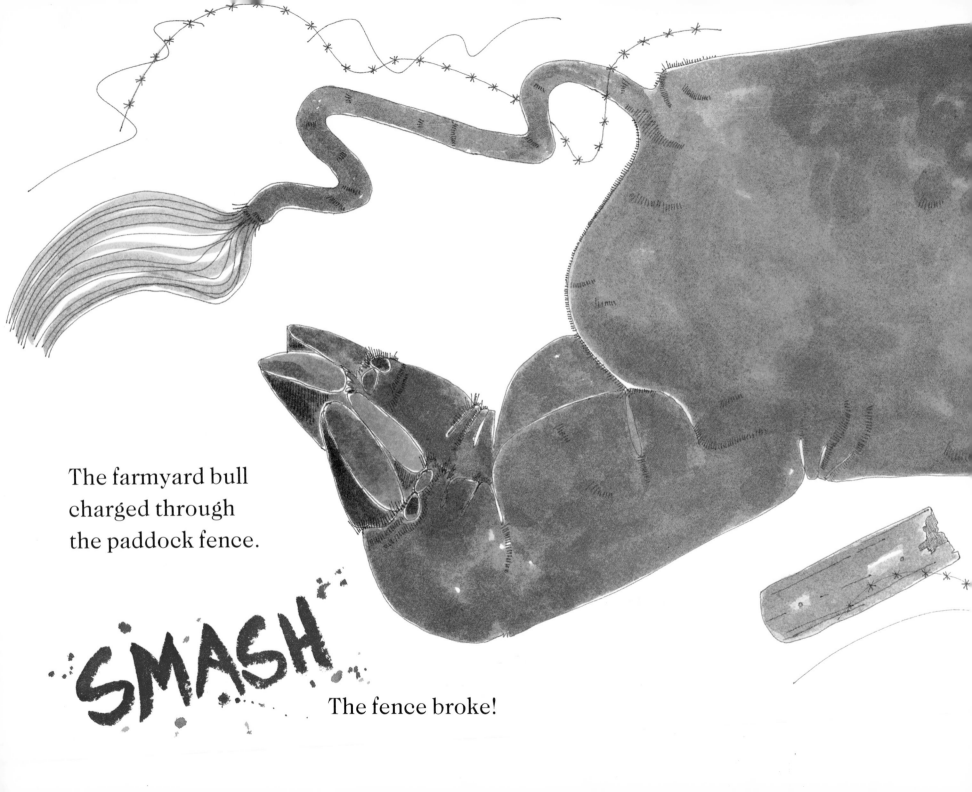

The farmyard bull
charged through
the paddock fence.

SMASH

The fence broke!

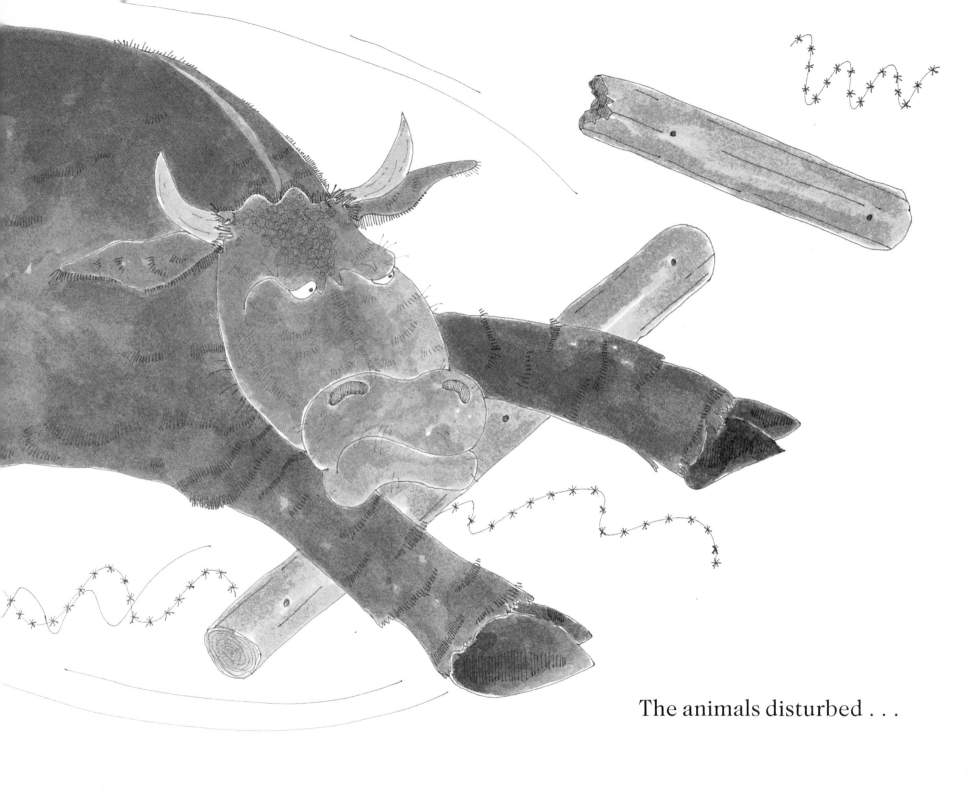

The animals disturbed . . .

. . . the farmyard nanny-goat.

The farmyard nanny-goat
was very angry.
She began to chase
the farmyard cat.

'I'll get you, cat!'
bleated the goat.
'I'll get you!'

The animals raced through the grassy paddock.

The farmyard cat ran through the legs . . .

. . . of the farmyard horse.

The farmyard horse was very angry.
He began to chase the farmyard cat.

'I'll get you, cat!'
snorted the horse.
'I'll get you!'

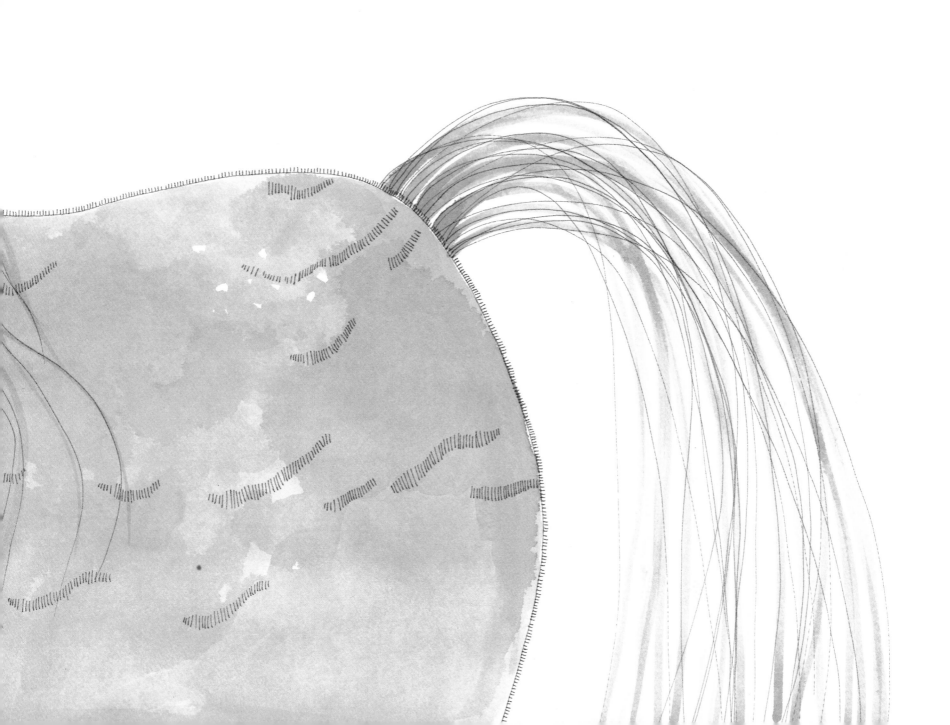

The animals were going too fast!
Suddenly . . .

. . . the farmyard cat stopped!

The farmyard animals
fell over the farmyard cat.
The farmyard animals
fell over each other.

They fell . . .

SPLOSH

into the muddy sty
of the farmyard pigs.

The farmyard cat
looked at all the muddy animals.
'How very clever I am!' she mewed.

The farmyard cat walked proudly away,
with her tail in the air.

'I got you animals.
I got you!' she purred.

'I got you ALL!'